To Suzanne Peters

"Studio of Music"

from

Lisa Gray

# Peter and the Wolf

Adapted from the Musical Tale by Sergei Prokofiev

## Illustrated by Erna Voigt

David R. Godine · Publisher · Boston

We hope that you will enjoy the story and illustrations in this book, but there is more to 'Peter and the Wolf' than words and pictures. The music which Sergei Prokofiev composed for this story has made it the most popular musical tale ever written for children.

Each character in the story is introduced by one of the instruments of the orchestra. Here they all are: Peter with the violin, Grandfather with the bassoon, the duck with the oboe, the cat with the clarinet and the wolf with the French horn. The hunters go rat-tat on the kettle drum and the little bird trills on the flute.

They all look friendly in this picture, but they are not such good friends when our story begins:

One morning, Peter opened the garden gate . . .

Violin

and walked out into the great, green meadow. Sitting
in a tree was Peter's friend, the little bird.

'All is quiet. All is well,'
chirped the bird happily as
Peter came to meet him.

Flute

Behind Peter waddled the duck. She was glad to see that Peter had not shut the gate, for now she could go and swim in the clear, blue pond which lay in the middle  of the meadow. When the little bird saw the duck swimming in the pond, he flew over and began to tease her.

'Call yourself a bird, when you can't even fly!' he taunted.

'Call yourself a bird, when you can't even swim!' quacked the duck, flapping her wings in annoyance.

Oboe

They were so busy quarrelling that neither of them noticed the cat slinking through the bushes. The cat was thinking, 'While they are arguing I shall creep up  on that bird and catch him!' Suddenly Peter saw the cat. 'Look out!' he shouted. The bird swooped up into the tree and the duck retreated to the middle of the pond and quacked crossly at the cat.

Clarinet

Just then Grandfather came out of the house. He was angry with Peter for leaving the garden gate open and  going into the meadow alone. 'The meadow is a dangerous place,' he said. 'What would you have done if a wolf had come out of the forest?' He took Peter back into the garden and closed the gate firmly.

Bassoon

No sooner had Peter left the meadow than a large grey  wolf did come creeping out of the forest. The cat ran quickly up into a tree.

French Horn

The duck squawked nervously and came rushing out
of the pond. The wolf saw her and began to chase her.
 How ever fast the poor duck
ran he came nearer and nearer
and then snapped her up and
swallowed her!

Oboe

Then the wolf peered up into the tree, where the cat was sitting on one branch, and the bird on another —  not too close. The wolf paced around the tree, staring hungrily at them.

Meanwhile, Peter, who had seen everything and was not at all frightened of the wolf, had run into the house to fetch some rope.

Violin

Peter climbed onto a branch of the tree, saying to the  little bird, 'Flutter round the wolf's nose — but don't let him catch you!'

The little bird fluttered and flapped, and try as he might the wolf could not catch him.

Flute

Peter made a loop at the end of his rope and lowered it

carefully over the wolf's tail.
Then he pulled the loop tight
and the wolf was trapped! The
wolf began to leap about, trying to free
himself, but Peter had tied the other end of
the rope to the tree, and the wolf's
struggles only pulled the loop tighter.

Violin

Just then three hunters came through the forest, firing  their guns. They were follow-
ing the trail of the wolf.
'Look, he went this way!' they
cried, and fired their guns again — bang!
bang! bang!

Kettle Drum

But Peter called down from his tree, 'Why are you shooting? The little bird and I have already caught the wolf!'

Kettle Drum

So they all set off in a triumphant procession to take
the wolf to the zoo. Peter led the way, followed by
 the hunters. Then came
Grandfather, shaking his
head and muttering, 'Suppose
Peter had not caught the wolf? What
would have happened then?'
The little bird flew overhead chirping
merrily, and if you listened very carefully
you could hear the duck quacking inside
the wolf's stomach. In his greed the wolf
had swallowed her whole, and she was
still alive!

Oboe

First U.S. edition published in 1980 by

David R. Godine, Publisher, Inc.
306 Dartmouth Street, Boston, Massachusetts 02116

Original title *Peter und der Wolf*, illustrations by Erna Voigt
Copyright © 1979 by Annette Betz Verlag, Vienna and Munich

ISBN 0-87923-331-1
LC 79-92902

Printed in Austria